W9-AAZ-036

DISCARD

**Green Light Readers
Harcourt, Inc.**

Orlando   Austin   New York

San Diego   London

# The Van

## Holly Keller

Sam has a van.

Pam sat in the van.

Max sat, too.

Dan sat in the van.

Pat sat, too.

Can the van go?

No!

Jan can help.

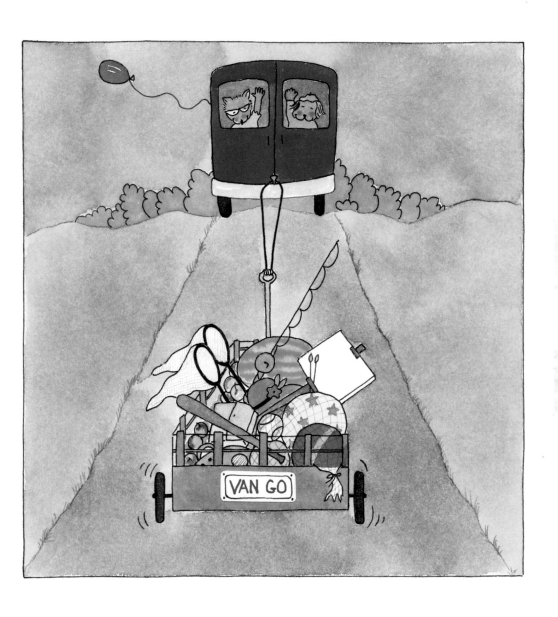

Now the van can go.

## What Do You Think?

Where do you think the animals in this story are going? Why do you think that?

Make a list of the things the animals take with them on their adventure.

If you were going with them, what would you want to take? Make another list.

Pretend you and your friends will ride in a van to your favorite place. Where will you go?

What will you take with you?

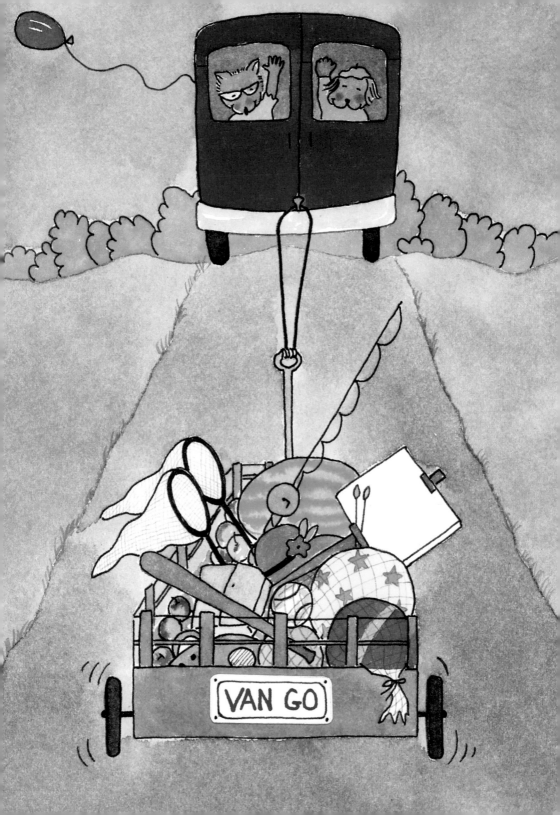

# What Will Happen?

You can make predictions about a story.

Use what you learn from the story and what you know from real life.

Look at these pictures.

You can use what you see and what you know. You can predict that the girl will probably take a bite of her food.

Look at these pictures. Tell what might happen next. Why do you think so?

## Try This!

Look at the pictures. Draw a picture to show what you think will happen next.

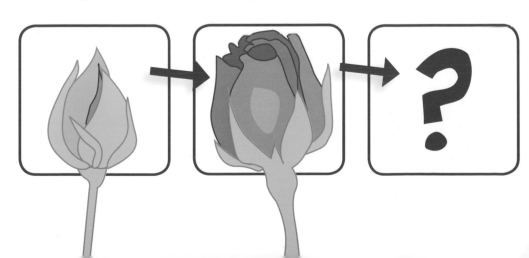

## Meet the Author-Illustrator
# Holly Keller

Holly Keller loves to draw animals
doing things that people might do.
She never had any pets growing up
but says animals are more fun to
draw. She gets her story ideas from
things she did as a child and things
her own children did. She says that
children's lives are full of stories.

Requests for permission to make copies of any part of the work should be submitted
online at www.harcourt.com/contact or mailed to the following address:
Permissions Department, Houghton Mifflin Harcourt Publishing Company,
6277 Sea Harbor Drive, Orlando, Florida 32887-6777.

www.HarcourtBooks.com

First Green Light Readers edition 2008

*Green Light Readers* and its logo are trademarks of Harcourt, Inc.,
registered in the United States of America and/or other jurisdictions.

Library of Congress Cataloging-in-Publication Data
Keller, Holly.
The van/Holly Keller.
p.  cm.
"Green Light Readers."
Summary: A family runs into difficulty when preparing for a trip in their van.
[1. Vans—Fiction.]  I. Title.
PZ7.K28132Van  2008
[E]—dc22  2007042341
ISBN 978-0-15-206577-5
ISBN 978-0-15-206587-4 (pb)

A C E G H F D B
A C E G H F D B (pb)

**Ages 4–6**
**Grade: 1**
**Guided Reading Level: B**
**Reading Recovery Level: 2**

# Green Light Readers
## For the reader who's ready to GO!

"A must-have for any family with a beginning reader."—*Boston Sunday Herald*

"You can't go wrong with adding several copies of these terrific books to your beginning-to-read collection."—*School Library Journal*

"A winner for the beginner."—*Booklist*

## Five Tips to Help Your Child Become a Great Reader

**1.** Get involved. Reading aloud to and with your child is just as important as encouraging your child to read independently.

**2.** Be curious. Ask questions about what your child is reading.

**3.** Make reading fun. Allow your child to pick books on subjects that interest her or him.

**4.** Words are everywhere—not just in books. Practice reading signs, packages, and cereal boxes with your child.

**5.** Set a good example. Make sure your child sees YOU reading.

## Why Green Light Readers Is the Best Series for Your New Reader

• Created exclusively for beginning readers by some of the biggest and brightest names in children's books

• Reinforces the reading skills your child is learning in school

• Encourages children to read—and finish—books by themselves

• Offers extra enrichment through fun, age-appropriate activities unique to each story

• Incorporates characteristics of the Reading Recovery program used by educators

• Developed with Harcourt School Publishers and credentialed educational consultants